Here Comes Trouble

TESSA KRAILING

Illustrated by Jan Lewis

Oxford University Press

Oxford University Press, Great Clarendon Street, Oxford OX2 6DP

Oxford   New York
Athens   Auckland   Bangkok   Bogota   Bombay
Buenos Aires   Calcutta   Cape Town   Dar es Salaam
Delhi   Florence   Hong Kong   Istanbul   Karachi
Kuala Lumpur   Madras   Madrid   Melbourne
Mexico City   Nairobi   Paris   Singapore
Taipei   Tokyo   Toronto   Warsaw

and associated companies in
Berlin   Ibadan

Oxford is a trade mark of Oxford University Press

Printed in Great Britain by Ebenezer Baylis

Illustrations by Jan Lewis

Photograph of Tessa Krailing by courtesy of Chris Thwaites

Chapter 1

On Friday afternoon Class Seven had an Art lesson. It was their favourite lesson of the week. Everyone looked forward to it.

Everyone except Trudy Hubble.

Trudy had elbows that stuck out and knocked things over. Her hands were large and clumsy. Her feet were so big she was always tripping over things.

When she came into the classroom Rob Mason said, 'Look out, here comes Trouble!'

This was Rob's idea of a joke. He called her 'Trouble' because it sounded like her two names – Trudy Hubble – put together. The other kids laughed. Trudy had to smile and pretend she didn't mind.

But she did mind. She minded a lot.

Mrs Weston said, 'Sit down, Trudy.
Let Lisa bring you a water jar and
some paints.'

...And DON'T MOVE
OUT OF YOUR SEAT
unless you must.

Trudy knew why Mrs Weston
wanted her to sit down. Mrs Weston
had been her teacher for three months
now. She had seen what happened
when Trudy tried to do Art. It was
always a disaster!

Lisa Gibbs fetched
paper and paint and
brushes.

She put them on the table she
shared with Trudy. Next, she filled a
jar with water and took that to Trudy.
Before she sat down she moved her
chair as far away from Trudy as
possible.

Trudy wished she could be more like
Lisa. Lisa never knocked things over.
She had small hands and feet and
wavy brown hair. Trudy's hair was as
straight as straw.

'Now today,' Mrs Weston said, 'I'd like you to paint me a monster. The scariest monster you can think of.'

'Oh, great!' Class Seven loved painting monsters.

Trudy decided to start with the eyes. The eyes were the scariest part of any monster. She dipped her brush in red paint. Then she made two large red circles on the paper.

Then two large yellow circles.

Then two large green circles.

But it didn't look much like a monster. It looked more like two sets of traffic lights.

She glanced at Lisa's picture. Lisa had painted a beautiful green dragon with flames coming out of its mouth.

Trudy sighed. She reached out to dip her brush in some black paint and – oh, no!

She knocked over the jam jar. Dirty water spread in a pool across the table. It drowned Lisa's dragon.

'Oops, sorry,' Trudy muttered. Lisa stared down at her soggy picture. Tears came into her eyes.

Rob Mason came over to look. 'Hey, Mrs Weston!' he called. 'Come and see what Trudy's done now.'

Trudy went red in the face. 'I'll get a cloth,' she muttered.

She jumped to her feet – and –

CRASH!

Her chair fell over backwards.

She turned round and her paintbrush caught Rob Mason across the face. It gave him a droopy black moustache.

He was so surprised that he staggered back against a wire bookstand. The bookstand came crashing down and books went all over the floor.

'Oh, no!' Mrs Weston came hurrying over. She caught her leg on Trudy's chair and laddered her tights.

Chapter 2

I hate Art, Trudy thought as she went
home on the bus. And I hate school!
She wished she never had to go to
school again.

The bus stopped outside her house.
She jumped up from her seat. Her
elbow knocked a woman's hat right
over her eyes.

Oops, sorry.

She got off the bus and ran indoors.
As soon as she opened the door she
knew something was wrong. The
house was too quiet. Not a sound from
the kitchen. Not a sound in the hall.
'Mum?' she called.

'I'm upstairs, Trudy.' Mum's voice sounded strange, all hoarse and croaky.

Trudy went upstairs two-at-a-time. She opened the bedroom door.

aaatchooo!

Mum lay in bed, holding a box of paper hankies. 'I've got an awful cold,' she said. 'Don't come too close or you might catch it.'

'Okay.' Trudy stayed near the door. 'Shall I make you a mug of tea?'

Mum said quickly, 'No, thanks. I'll wait till your dad gets home.'

Trudy sighed. She knew why Mum didn't want her to make any tea. She was afraid Trudy would spill it coming up the stairs.

... But there is something I'd like you to do, Sniff.

'What's that?' Trudy asked eagerly.

'Take a message to Mrs Willow. Tell her I shan't be well enough to come to work tomorrow.' Mum blew her nose into a paper hanky. 'She's a very old lady. I don't want to give her my cold.'

Trudy turned to the door.
'Thanks. Oh, but Trudy –'
Trudy stopped. 'Yes, Mum?'

'Mrs Willow's house is full of beautiful things. I have to be very, very careful not to break anything. So, if she asks you to come in, you'd better say no.'

Trudy sighed. 'Yes, Mum.'

She went downstairs again and ran along the crowded street. 'Oops, sorry,' she said as she bumped into a passer-by.

Luckily she didn't have far to go.

Mrs Willow lived in a tall, graceful old house. Trudy knocked on the door and waited. She heard the tap-tap of a stick coming from inside.

The door opened.

There stood an old lady with white hair and sharp blue eyes. Although she walked with a stick, she was tall and graceful, like her house.

'Hello, Mrs Willow,' said Trudy. 'I'm Trudy Hubble. My mum's your home help. She won't be able to come tomorrow. She's got a cold.'

'I'm sorry to hear that. What she needs is my special cold cure. Come inside and I'll give you some.' Mrs Willow opened the door wider.

Trudy remembered her mother's warning. 'I'll wait here,' she said.

'Nonsense, you can wait in my sitting room.' Mrs Willow turned and started to walk down the hall, her stick tap-tapping on the floor.

Oh, help! thought Trudy. What should she do?

'Come in, come in,' called Mrs Willow.

Trudy took a deep breath and stepped inside.

Chapter 3

Trudy looked round Mrs Willow's sitting room.

She saw at once why Mum had been worried. There were beautiful things everywhere – pretty china figures and little glass animals, delicate tea sets and glass bowls. But the most beautiful thing of all stood alone on a little table. It was a large green-and-white vase with a dragon painted on the side.

Trudy stood very, very still. She was afraid to move in case she knocked something over. Stiff as a statue, she kept her elbows pressed to her sides.

Mrs Willow came back into the room. 'Ah, I see you're looking at my Chinese vase,' she said. 'It's very, very old. Do you like it?'

Trudy nodded.

Mrs Willow held out a small brown bottle. 'Here's my cold cure,' she said. 'Don't ask me what's in it. It's an old family secret. But it always works.'

Trudy took the bottle. She couldn't speak because she was holding her breath.

Mrs Willow looked hard at her. 'Is something wrong?'

Trudy shook her head.

'But you've gone quite red in the face. Are you sure you're all right?'

Trudy could hold her breath no longer. She let it out in a long, long sigh. 'I'm fine,' she said. 'Thanks for the cold cure, Mrs Willow. I must go home now.'

Mrs Willow looked sad. 'Can't you stay for a cup of tea?'

'No, I – I have to go.'

Trudy couldn't wait to get away. The room was too full of beautiful things. Any minute now there would be a disaster, she felt sure. She turned to the door.

Something furry brushed against her leg. Trudy jumped backwards.

The furry thing gave a loud
'YEOWLL!' It leaped on to the piano.

Trudy jumped again, sideways. Her
elbow hit the green-and-white vase. It
began to sway. She watched in horror
as it rocked from side to side...

...to side to side...

...to side to side and...

CRASH!

It fell to the floor and broke into little pieces. DISASTER.

Nobody moved. The cat – who had caused all the trouble – sat on top of the piano. It swished its tail.

Then Trudy said, 'Oh, I'm sorry. I'm really sorry. It's because I'm clumsy. That's why I didn't want to come into your house. I knew something would get broken. It always does when I'm around.'

'It's all right,' Mrs Willow said calmly.

It doesn't matter.

Surprised, Trudy stared at her.

Doesn't matter?

'Not a bit. You see, that vase has been broken before. It had to be mended then. And do you know who broke it?' Mrs Willow smiled. 'I did, when I was just about your age. Yes, I used to be clumsy too.'

Trudy couldn't believe it. Mrs Willow seemed so tall and graceful. She didn't look the sort of person who would knock things over.

'You couldn't have been as clumsy as I am,' she said.

I'm the clumsiest person in our school!

Mrs Willow took a photo from the top of the piano. 'Do you see this girl playing tennis?' she asked. 'Well, that was me.'

Trudy looked at the photo.

The girl playing tennis was tall and thin with untidy hair. She had a wide grin on her face.

Mrs Willow laughed. 'I was a real ugly duckling, wasn't I? But do you remember what happened to the ugly duckling?'

Trudy nodded. 'It grew up to be a swan. But I don't think I shall. I'll just grow up to be an ugly duck.'

'Not if you do as I did. You have to keep telling yourself that inside, where it matters, you're really a swan.'

Trudy said doubtfully, 'I'm a swan.'

'It does work, you know. It's a kind of magic. Say it again. This time, as if you really believe it.'

Trudy cleared her throat. She said it louder.

Mrs Willow smiled. 'Now help me clear up these bits of old vase. Then we'll have some tea.'

They drank tea from china cups.
They ate chocolate cake off delicate
plates.

And Trudy didn't break another
thing. She ran home muttering, 'I'm a
swan, I'm a swan,' and she didn't
bump into a single person. So perhaps
it was a kind of magic, after all.

But what would happen tomorrow,
when she went to school?

Chapter 4

Next morning Mum's cold was much
better. 'That's because of Mrs Willow's
secret family cure,' Trudy said.

'It tastes horrible,' said Mum.
'But it seems to work.'

Trudy was glad the cold cure had
worked. It proved that Mrs Willow
knew what she was talking about. And
if the cold cure worked, then the swan
cure might work as well. She couldn't
wait to try it out.

On the way to school she tried
thinking herself a swan.

She glided on to the bus and sat
down slowly. She didn't trip over
anyone's feet. She didn't knock
anyone's hat off.

When the bus stopped, she rose
slowly from her seat.

She stepped on to
the pavement.

It was surprising how different she
felt, so tall and graceful.

In the school playground some
children stood looking up into the
chestnut tree.

'Look out, here comes Trouble!'
called Rob Mason when he saw her.

Trudy pretended not to hear him.
She saw that Lisa Gibbs was in tears.
'What's the matter?' she asked.

'It's Lisa's kite,' said Rob. 'It's got stuck up the tree.'

'Rob did it,' Lisa said, wiping her eyes. 'He let go and it flew up into the tree.'

Rob looked a bit ashamed of himself. 'Stupid old kite,' he muttered.

'It's a beautiful kite!' said Lisa. 'I got it for my birthday. It was my best present.' She began to sob again.

'Don't cry,' Trudy said kindly. 'I'll get it down for you. I'm good at climbing trees.'

Lisa looked horrified. 'No, you'll tear it! It's only made of paper. Can't somebody else get it down?'

But nobody else wanted to climb the tree.

Trudy jumped up and grabbed the lowest branch. She swung herself up and began to climb.

'Be careful,' called Lisa. 'It's a special Chinese kite. It cost a lot of money.'

Like the vase, Trudy thought, and nearly stopped. But then she thought of Mrs Willow.

'I'm a swan, I'm a swan,' she muttered.

And she started climbing again. She climbed higher and higher until she reached the kite.

The kite was caught on a sharp twig. It was made of thin, silky paper and had a green dragon painted on it. Don't rush, she told herself. Swans never rush.

At last she managed to free
the kite.

But now she had to climb down
again using only one hand. It took
her ages, but she didn't rush.

She saw that Mrs Weston had
joined the crowd below. But she
still didn't rush.

Very, very carefully she swung
herself down to the ground.

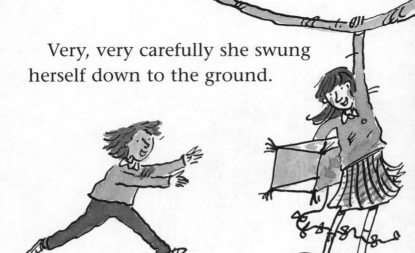

The kite was safe!
'Thanks, Trudy.' Lisa showed it to
the others. 'Look, it's all right!'

She didn't
tear it after all!

Trudy felt very, very proud. But then
Mrs Weston said, 'Trudy Hubble, what
a mess you look! Your hands and knees
are filthy. Go and wash them AT
ONCE!'

For a moment Trudy felt like her old
clumsy self. But then she remembered
what Mrs Willow had said. It didn't
matter how she looked outside.
Inside, she was really
a swan.

Trudy smiled at
Mrs Weston. Then
she glided swan-like across the
playground and into school.

About the author

I wrote my first story at the age of four. From that moment I knew I wanted to be a writer, but it was many years before my first book (which was about dinosaurs) was published. Since then I have written over thirty books for children of all ages.

This story is really about a girl I used to teach. She was very clumsy and often knocked her paint water over in Art lessons, just like Trudy. But she grew up to be a graceful ballet dancer.